To Tell a Tale or Two

16 short stories

By Kelly Florentia

Copyright
Kelly Florentia © 2014

All characters, names and events in this book are fictitious. All stories have been created from the author's imagination. Any resemblance to any real persons, living or dead, is entirely coincidental.

All rights reserved

Contents

Band of Gold 4

For Ruby's Sake 9

Waiting for Daisy 14

Greek Connection 20

A Passionate Crime 30

The Client 36

Heavenly Scent 41

Table Manners 47

Never Let You Go 55

My Girl 61

First Date Escape 66

Open Wide 72

No Way Back 78

The Accident 83

The Visitor 88

I Heart You 97

BAND OF GOLD

I twist the top off the tester pot of eye cream and give it a quick sniff. *'Reduces puffiness and wrinkles'*, it promises on the exclusive looking label. Well, it better had at £64.50 per 15ml pot. I wasn't intending on buying it, of course. My usual one only costs £8.99 from the local supermarket. But I was surprisingly captivated by her charm. She was quite different from the usual beauty consultants in this store – warm, pleasant, unassuming.

"Are you looking for anything in particular?" She smiles kindly, her brown eyes meet mine. I give her face a quick scan desperately looking for imperfections but find none.

"I need something for these," I say with half a smile, pointing to the crow's feet and dark circles under my eyes, that she'd helped put there. As she reaches for my face across the tall highly stacked counter, I quiver, and she frowns, concerned.

"Just tired eyes," she says in a friendly professional tone, drawing her hand back, clearly not wanting to invade my personal space. How very thoughtful of her. "But if you'd like something to ward off the appearance of wrinkles while combating puffy eyes, I'd recommend this." She runs a French manicured hand down the neat display shelf, hovers at the forties range, glances at me quickly, then moves her hand down a decade. Then just as she turns to face me I picture them together and my stomach twists.

"It was just the once, Rebecca," James had said, when I found a string of intimate text messages on his mobile phone a week ago. "I swear." He clutched his chest, "Cross my heart. And *she* came onto me," he said defiantly. As if that was supposed to make it less of an injustice.

"You were supposed to turn her down, James," I yelled tearfully, "You've got a wife, remember?" I prized off my wedding ring and hurled it at him.

"You never take that off," he said quietly, looking hurt.

"Unlike you!" I retorted. James has never worn his ring, claims he's allergic to gold but now I know different.

The beauty consultant gives me a sideward glance, her red luscious lips curling into a lopsided grin. "This works wonders," she says excitedly; and with a doubtful expression, I take the slim tube from her elegant hand and tell her she's too young for wrinkles, surely she doesn't need it. "Oooh, yes I do," she whispers, "I'm thirty-six next week!"

I raise an eyebrow. "You look so much younger." She looks a good ten years younger, but I feel a slither of comfort at this disclosure, at least she's not the twenty-something babe that I'd imagined.

"Give me some of that cream right now," I grin, forgetting for a moment that she's the enemy. I lick my dry lips hesitatingly. This is completely insane. I can't believe that I'm standing in the middle of a busy department store sharing a joke with a woman who's ruining my marriage.

Tracking her down was a doddle. James has never been very good at covering things up, which is how I found out in the first place, of course.

"Andrew knows," he said, later that evening when things had quietened down. "He may have told Kate too," he added with a cringe. I pushed the glass of wine away from me angrily, almost knocking it off the table. I could just about handle his best friend knowing but not the entire crowd. I felt sick, humiliated, betrayed.

"I want you to leave," I said, leaping to my feet. "Now!" And I meant it. But he managed to woo me with his charm. Begged me for another chance. Told me that he loved me desperately. That he couldn't live without me.

"Please don't throw away three years of marriage over a drunken one-night-stand," he pleaded. But I couldn't even look at him. "We could start afresh, try for a baby," he said eagerly. I glanced at him, my spirits momentarily lifting. I'd been trying to persuade him to start a family since we first got married.

"I don't know, James." I bit on my lips, folding my arms.

"Please, Rebecca, I really mean it. Can you just imagine, a little mini you and me?" He looked at me, his dark eyes full of remorse and I felt myself soften.

"I need time to think," I said finally. I wanted to believe him because despite everything, I knew that I still loved him. You can't turn love on and off like a light switch, can you? But I had to see her first. The urgency to see who she was, what she looked like, what made her so irresistible to my husband was overpowering. The next morning I rang Kate at the office.

"I'm so sorry, Rebecca," she said gravely, "Andrew said they met in the Dog and Hound across the road from our office. She's a beauty therapist of some sort. Works in the department store next door."

So, here I am. Face to face with my adversary. My future in her hands, or hers in mine.

"This one's a bit expensive." I crinkle my nose.

"Hmm..." She frowns for a moment, then her eyes light up with excitement, "I know just the one, but it's on the shelf beside you." And as she moves away from the counter and I see her for the first time in full view, I feel my legs give slightly. I steady myself against a black leather barstool.

"This is magical," she beams, holding a long white tube to my face. Suddenly everything seems surreal. I feel lightheaded, detached, as if I'm standing on a bouncy castle.

"When's it due?" I ask, forcing a smile.

"Oh, not for another five months," she whines. I tell myself that it could be someone else's. James swore it was a recent one-night-stand. She might have a string of lovers for all I know. I regain my composure.

"Bet your partner's happy," I open my red leather purse as she packs the eye cream into a tiny pink paper bag with delicate straw handles.

"Ex," she says with a sad smile. "He's married. It's complicated." She must sense my disapproval because she quickly adds, "I only found out last week. Doesn't wear a ring, you see, reckons he's allergic to gold. More fool me, hey?" She says, her words closing in around me, sealing my fate.

"I'm so sorry," I say, swallowing hard. And I mean it. Not just for her, but for us.

FOR RUBY'S SAKE

I bonded with Ruby the moment she was born. The very second I looked into her big brown eyes – I was smitten. Perhaps it was because I was only sixteen at the time, unaware of the difficulties that lay ahead.

It was different when Jamie and Ryan came along. I was older, more mature. I was able to discipline them, set rules, curfews. Don't get me wrong, I love my boys with all my heart and soul. But with Ruby it was different.

"You're too soft with her, Luisa," my sister, Amanda, would often remark while Ruby was growing up.

"Shush, you," I'd reply, "You know she's my special girl." And I'd wink at Ruby and she'd wink back, our special sign.

And now here I am, in this disarray with Ruby, unable to do anything to help her, except offer my support. This isn't a grazed knee, low GCSE grades or boyfriend trouble. This is much more complicated.

My stomach stirs, which isn't surprising given that I've barely eaten or slept during the last few days. I check my mobile phone for any missed calls or texts from Amanda but my screen is empty.

"I don't want you to tell a living soul," Ruby had pleaded two weeks ago when she'd found out. "Promise me!"

"What, not even…"

"Especially not her," she cut in quickly, reading my thoughts. But Ruby knew that Amanda and I told each other everything, that we were best friends as well as sisters.

"You can tell her when it's all over," Ruby said finally, threading her fingers through her dark, thick curls and sighing. "She'll only interfere if you tell her now. You know what she's like." And I did. Amanda was too soft. Saw everything through rose-tinted glasses. I was more stoic, methodical, able to deal with life's difficulties head on, whereas she usually fell apart at the first hurdle. I often picked up the pieces after my older sister.

"Okay," I sighed. "I promise I won't breathe a word."

And somehow we managed to get through the two-week hospital wait. I had to stay strong, for Ruby's sake.

A blue-uniformed nurse rustles past and I slip my mobile phone back into my handbag quickly.

"Everything okay?" she smiles.

"I hope so," I croak nervously, clearing my throat. "How long will she be?"

"The doctor's with her now. Try not to worry – she'll be fine. She's a strong girl. You've done a great job." I smile awkwardly. I can't bear this any longer. I know I promised, but I need Amanda.

Amanda answers the phone in her usual chirpy tone. When I tell her about Ruby I hear the alarm in her voice instantly.

"What? When? Why didn't you tell me?" I knew she'd react like this. Ruby was right.

"Ruby didn't want me to…"

"I'm on my way," she cuts in quickly, then hangs up abruptly.

When I return to the unit I get a glimpse of Ruby in a blue and white gown coming out of the Day Treatment section and my heart surges. Then she catches my eye and winks, and as I wink back a big fat tear splashes from my eye and rolls down my face. Soon she's dressed and back in my arms.

"All over?" I ask.

"Yes," she says, faintly, "all done."

I tell her that I've rang Amanda and that she's on her way. "Please, Ruby," I say softly, "I had to tell her, she's my sister."

"Okay, okay." She waves a hand. "Honestly, you two are joined at the hip." She shakes her head, smiling. "You know she would've flipped over this, don't you?" I nod quickly, staring at my feet. "She'd have insisted on coming along and embarrassed us in front of the hospital staff, driven us all mad, as usual." I smile sympathetically but we both know that this isn't the reason for her absence. Ruby has a wonderful relationship with Amanda.

"And *you* know how much she loves you, Ruby," I protest, "It' just her way of dealing with things, that's all." I ruffle her hair, so thankful that she's okay. That she managed to get through this ordeal. Our moment is punctured by the sound of a commotion drifting rapidly towards us.

"I'm sorry," says a flustered nurse. We both look round. Amanda is here, looking frazzled. "I couldn't stop her, she insists she's your…"

"It's okay," I cut in. Amanda's eyes are red and puffy. Her hair is held up unevenly with numerous clips, and she's still wearing her pink slippers.

"Ruby," Amanda manages through trembling lips, "what's going on?"

"Oh, Mum," Ruby gulps, "I'm so sorry. I didn't want to worry you."

"But a breast lump, Ruby, you're only twenty-six." Ruby blinks back the tears, restlessly scrabbling through her bag.

"It was a benign cyst, Mum." She looks up into Amanda's eyes and then falls into her arms. "I had it aspirated," she mumbles, sobbing into her mother's shoulder. "The doctor said it's nothing to worry about, quite a few young women get them but I was really scared, Mum. If it wasn't for Auntie Luisa I....." Amanda lets out a loud sigh of relief, stroking her daughter's hair lovingly.

"Thanks for being here, Luisa." She reaches out for me and I join them in a group hug. "And for letting me know."

After a few moments, we disentangle and Amanda pulls out a tissue from her coat pocket.

"Come on." She blows her nose loudly, "Let's go home." We all grab our bags. "And you two," she says, shaking the crumpled tissue at us, "had better promise me right now that you're not to keep anything like this from me again."

"Never again," I promise, stretching my arms around my big sister and niece, "And I do love your choice of footwear, darling, perfect for this time of year, *Manolos,* are they?" We look down at Amanda's pink fluffy slippers. Amanda elbows me gently in the ribs and grins while Ruby glows the colour of her name.

"Oh Mum," Ruby groans. "You always manage to show me up."

WAITING FOR DAISY

"Great seats," says Tanya, settling into her red velvet chair, her eyes sparkling with anticipation. 'Hope he chooses one of us." She hoists her shoulders excitedly. I'm not quite sure what I'm doing here, to be honest, psychic demonstrations isn't my thing. But I couldn't pass up on the chance of seeing him again.

"An evening of clairvoyance with Steven Van-Hamilton," Tanya had said, a few weeks ago, staring at the local newspaper sprawled on her desk, "Rob won't go, how about you, Jan?"

At first I said *no*, but then when she showed me his photograph I felt the colour drain from my face. He'd changed his name, his hair had receded and greyed, but he still had that killer smile that melted my heart fifteen years ago.

"Yeah, go on then," I said, regaining my composure, "it might be a laugh." And without hesitation she booked two seats with a few clicks of her mouse.

The local theatre is heaving. I close my eyes and roll back the years to the last time we saw each other. I'd just told him that I was pregnant. I thought he'd be happy.

"Get rid of it," he demanded. When I told him that I wouldn't, he went into a rage. Pressing his foot down on the accelerator, he swerved around the bends at top speed.

"Slow down," I cried, "you're going to kill us." But he just kept going faster and faster. The next thing I knew I was on a hospital bed with a drip in my arm.

The thought of it still sends shivers down my spine, and then Steven Van-Hamilton walks onto the stage to a roar of applause, shaking me out of my reverie.

Half an hour later he has the audience captivated.

"Aha, yeah, ok, I'll tell her," he says, staring into space, and then delivers a heartfelt message to a grateful lady in the front row. The crowd seem to hang onto his every word. Just what he'd always wanted - fame and adulation. "I have a young boy with me." He squints and points in our direction, "I'm drawn to this row here." Then he clocks me and our eyes lock.

"He's looking at you," Tanya whispers excitedly, nudging me on the arm. I feel the bile rise into my chest.

"I can't do this, Tanya, sorry." I stand up. Sighs and tuts echo in my ears as I sway and stumble through a sea of legs. Then I bolt for the exit. Tanya follows behind me, while Steven-Van-Hamilton tells his audience that he'll be back after a twenty-minute interval.

"Are you all right?" Tanya frowns, staring at the supper I had this evening on the pavement. "Did you eat something dodgy?" I look up – Steven is standing behind her.

"Jan," he says softly, "I thought it was you."

"What the...? Do you two know each other?"

"Please," he says, "give us a few moments."

Tanya looks at me, eyes wide with concern. I nod, still holding my stomach. "I'll be in the bar," she says, giving Steven a dubious sideward glance, "if you need me."

"Come on." Steven leads me gently by the arm to his tiny dressing room behind the set. He pours me a shot of vodka. "Here, it'll help with the shock." I knock it back in one. "You look great, Jan."

"No thanks to you," I retort, smoothing down my black sweater. "I hear that you're happily married now with kids."

He nods slowly, his face red. "We were too young, Jan." He stares at his expensive looking shoes. "Things were just starting to take off for me. Then after the accident, well, I just had to get away." There's an awkward silence punctured by loud voices coming from the corridor - laughing, joking, swearing. "I'm sorry about the baby." He exhales loudly.

"They were twins," I say dryly, but he can't even look at me. "Anyway, thanks for the drink." I head for the door, he grabs my arm.

"You will have another child, Jan..... a girl." I follow his eyes over my shoulder. He's staring into thin air. "She'll look just like you but she'll have the name of your partner's mother. Daisy," he smiles, eyes bright. "She's been a long wait but worth it."

I shake my head incredulously. Is this the best that he can do after all the hurt he's caused? Am I supposed to forget all about the past and just go home and wait for Daisy?

I want to tell him that he's talking rubbish. That Peter's mum is called Joan, and that our plans don't include any children.

"Save it, Steven," I say tightly, "for someone who cares."

I close the door behind me. No longer angry, just relived that I've finally put the past to rest.

I feel giddy when the cold evening air hits me, but thankfully Tanya is driving. Then I hear his voice again.

"Jan." He pushes a piece of paper into my pocket. "If you ever need me." Then he turns on his heel and quickly runs up the theatre steps.

"Come on, Tanya." I say, "I've seen enough ghosts for one evening, let's go."

At home, I collapse onto the sofa and kick off my shoes, then wrap my arms around Peter.

"Good night?" he asks." Tom's just gone up to bed. Fancy a cuppa?"

"Oooh, yes please." I say, rubbing my tired toes.

I take Steven's note from my pocket. '*So sorry I've been an absent father, call me if you need anything.*' I feel my face flush as a multitude of thoughts race through my mind. Surely, he can't be for real? Of course not, I reason. Someone must've told him that I'd only lost one of the twins. All he had to do was call the hospital.

"Jan? You ok?"

I stare into Peter's blue eyes. "Absolutely," I say, scrunching the paper into a ball and tossing it into the bin. "Cancel the tea, let's go to bed."

"You're on," he says, grinning.

"Daisy," I say to myself, gathering my shoes from the floor, "what absolute tosh."

"Oi, you, don't let my mum hear you say that."

"What?" I look up at him, shocked. "Joan?"

"Joan's her middle name and one she seems to prefer, but her first name is Daisy. I think it's rather lovely, don't you?"

GREEK CONNECTION

"A church wedding," says Mrs Papadakis in a heavy accent, placing a cup of Greek coffee onto the huge rustic table in front of me. I'm not quite sure whether this is a question or a statement. It does sound rather like a demand, to be honest, but Panos had warned me about his mother before we arrived.

"She's very patriotic, Tanya, and a bit set in her ways but she's a pussycat really, once you get to know her." I look at my future mother-in-law. The woman I've been longing to meet. The woman I want to make a good impression on.

"Coffee smells lovely," I offer, "just what I need to perk me up after that laborious flight."

They don't take their eyes off me as I draw the tiny cup to my lips. Goodness, I'm only sampling their local coffee not taking part in a bush tucker trial in the Australian jungle. I have drunk continental coffee before, you know. I'm not a flipping lightweight. I shake off their scrutiny and take a large sip with poise, but as the hot, dark liquid hits my tongue it feels like an explosion of caffeine in my mouth. I resist the urge to run to the sink. I daren't make such a scene on my first visit.

"Strong coffee," I manage, trying to swallow the thick, gritty liquid.

"It's unfiltered." Panos gives me a wry smile as he hands me a glass of ice-cold water, which I gulp down within seconds. "And an acquired taste," he adds with a wink. "A bit like Marmite."

Mrs Papadakis, who is standing by the stove with her arms crossed against her ample chest, doesn't look impressed. Grey strands of hair have escaped from her untidy bun. She blows them off her olive skin and looks at me expectantly.

"Oh, yes," I say finally, "Panos and I are happy with a church wedding."

Her face instantly creases into a smile as she throws her chubby arms up in delight and then folds them around me. I'm not used to hugging people I've only just met, but I make an exception and respond with a gentle hug and a light pat on the back.

"There is a condition though, Mrs Papadakis," I say, barely able to breathe from her tight embrace. We disentangle quickly and her dark eyes lock with mine. "It has to be held in London as I'd like all my family and friends to be there," I gasp. Thankfully, she approves and pulls up a chair next to mine.

We chat about her life in London. She tells me how she misses the city and what good times she had there.

"But when my husband die, what I could do?" she says in broken English. "A young woman with ten- year-old boy, by myself. I had to come home to family, you know." I nod sympathetically, and I know that she and I will get on just fine.

Three weeks later, Panos and I are enjoying a romantic meal in the old Venetian town of Chania, where lovers walk hand in hand, restaurants tucked in narrow alleyways spill onto pebble-stoned pavements and the sound of the bouzouki drones blissfully in the background. But instead of basking in the ambience, I find myself thinking about home. About Ben.

"Tanya, have you completely lost it?" Ben had said, flinging my resignation onto his desk in anger. "Giving up everything for a bloke you met on holiday with Stacey?" Ben's one of the company directors and, I hasten to add, my ex-boyfriend. He's gorgeous, charming and successful. He's also a compulsive flirt and commitment-phobe, you know the type.

"Ben, it's been nine months. Remember? " I got a swirl of satisfaction from watching him squirm at being reminded of his betrayal. I'd found several selfies of him and Emma from Accounts on his Blackberry, all cosied up on a four-poster hotel bed. "Besides," I went on, "I fly over to see Panos regularly. I've probably spent more time with him than I ever did with you."

But, surprisingly, Ben wasn't going to let go without a fight. He promised fidelity, confessed to not being able to get me out of his system. He even went as far as saying that I was 'the one'. But I wasn't born yesterday.

And then, to my astonishment, he did the unthinkable.

"Look, I know what this is all about." He held out his hand as if trying to defuse one of his confrontational clients, "and neither of us is getting any younger.... so, well...if you want, we could..."

"Ben, are you asking me to marry you?"

"Well…yes! I am if it'll make you stay." Hmm…not quite the proposal that I'd imagined. Not that I expected him to go down on one knee or anything as drastic as that. But come on, surely a girl deserved more than this?

Flowers, chocolates and love notes continued to arrive at my rented flat in Muswell Hill all week.

On the morning I was due to leave for Crete he turned up on my doorstep clutching a dozen red roses in one hand and a small Tiffany box in the other. Ben was no quitter.

"Don't, Ben," I said, pulling my dressing gown around me tightly. "If you'd asked me a year ago I might've said yes, but now it's too late."

"A vine picker," he snorted, "who lives in a shed with his mother?" Damn Stacey, she could never keep her mouth shut. "You're only doing this to spite me, aren't you?" he spat, "Admit it." He leant forward, his lips close to mine.

"No, Ben." I pushed him away. "The world doesn't revolve around you! It's over between us. I'm leaving." His steel blue eyes searched mine, but I didn't flinch.

"You'll never be able to rough it, Tanya," he huffed, backing away, "I'll give you three weeks tops before you start missing your home comforts." He hurled the lovely bouquet into the corner of my porch, forcing the red petals to scatter onto the stone patio - and then he was gone from my life. Until yesterday, that is, when his text appeared on my iPhone - *'missing u like crazy. R u ok? Pls call me xxx.'*

Ben was right, incidentally. Panos isn't well off. We live minimally in a rundown house in Agia Marina, and I'm finding it impossible to find a job. But I can see the shimmering sea from our bedroom window when I awake each morning, and feel the warmth of the sun massaging my back as I stroll to the local bakery for our fresh bread.

Okay, Panos can't give me the security or quality lifestyle that Ben could provide. But money isn't everything, is it? So, I'll never have that fairytale wedding I'd always dreamt of, or the lovely house with my own drive and picturesque garden. Nor will I have the luxury of long-haul holidays and romantic weekend breaks. I chew my bottom lip. Panos was on the rebound. But surely I know my own mind......don't I?

"Any regrets?" asks Panos, as if he could read my mind, "I know your missing home." I take a sip of red Makedonikos and stare into the distance, trying desperately to make sense of my tangled emotions. Ben did say Emma was a huge mistake, and he did try his best to win me back. Perhaps, I was hasty. Maybe I should've given him another chance. "We could move back to London once we're married," Panos goes on. "I speak English, I'm sure my uncle Andreas would give me a job in his restaurant and....." I cover his soft lips with my hand and look deep into his dark, brown eyes that are full of concern and confusion.

"Panos," I say gently, he kisses my fingertips softly, seductively, as the bouzouki player moves in to serenade us. "We need to talk."

The next morning we head off to the mountains to meet Panos' grandparents who've just returned from visiting relatives in Corfu. He takes the spiral, uneven roads at what seems like top speed. I thank God when we finally pull up outside an old derelict bungalow. I climb out of the open-topped truck feeling frazzled and nauseous, and step into a heap of manure.

"Oh no," I cry, "my Louboutins." Panos, laid back and easy going, says he'll buy me another pair. "Have you any idea how much these cost?" I growl, pointing the four-inch stiletto at him, "They were a gift from...from...oh, never mind!"

He shakes his head in exasperation as he disappears behind the truck, returning moments later with a pair of oversized sandals that'd probably been lurking there for centuries.

"You're hair looks nice like that, Tanya." He hands me the sandals.

"Are you having a laugh?" I wipe the smeared mascara from my cheekbones. "It was shiny and straight before we left home!" Thanks to the heat, humidity and wind, I'm now sporting an inelegant bouffant. What will his grandparents think of me? "And I'll only come up to your waist in these," I grumble, shaking the sandals at him. Okay, slight exaggeration but who cares? I'm angry. "I'm not happy, Panos." I complain, brushing down my new jeans hard and furious.

"Oh grow up, Tanya. They're just a pair of shoes, for goodness sake," he yells, "and I did warn you not to wear them". Great - our first fight and not a door in sight to slam. I glare at him but before I can hurl another insult his grandparents appear and Panos mouths, 'I'm sorry,' and I can't help but smile.

"This is my Yiayia," His frail little granny dressed in black from head to toe welcomes me with a hard kiss on both cheeks.

"And, Papou." The elderly man, fully clad in long black boots over traditional baggy trousers and black headscarf, takes my hand. "This is my Tanya." Granddad's thick, white moustache tickles my fingers as his dry lips brush against my hand, and thoughts about my appearance are quickly forgotten.

We sit outside their house on old wooden chairs that feel as though they are about to collapse beneath us as we sip Greek coffee, a taste I've come to acquire. I can't think of the last time that I felt so relaxed, so safe....so normal. I close my eyes, savouring the moment until my iPhone buzzes manically in my bag. I yank it out irritably. Ten messages, three missed calls, all from Ben. I swallow hard. I know what I have to do.....

When Panos tells his grandparents that we're getting married they leap off their seats in delight.

Within half an hour the house is jam-packed with guests, eating and drinking to our health and happiness. I've never known anyone with so many close relatives. I smile as Panos wraps his arms around me and sigh contently as I stretch my arms around his trim waist, and I know that I've made the right choice.

"Hey, sorry I fell asleep last night. You said you wanted to talk," he says blithely, his eyes sparkling with joy, "remember? " I wonder if I should tell him the truth. Confess that although hearing from Ben again stirred something inside me, I still chose him - a good, decent man who genuinely loved me over a rich, materialistic lothario who, deep down, only really loved himself.

"It was nothing," I whisper. Some things are best left unsaid. "It's sorted." I lean forward, my eyes close, our lips touch then a thunderous voice cries,

"Panos! Panos!" We pull apart quickly and follow his grandfather outside to where his granny is waiting. Away from the intoxication of the blaring music, dancing and laughter, I suddenly feel sober and alert. We face his grandparents, expectantly.

I can tell from his grandfather's tone and his grandma's expression that they're talking about something very serious. I frown anxiously, fist clenched, tension rising in my body.

"What are they saying, Panos?" I must learn to speak Greek.

"My Grandparents want to give us their property," he says through trembling lips. I sigh with relief, then look around their humble little home, tears stinging my eyes. They know that Panos and I are struggling financially but this gesture is beyond generous.

"THANK. YOU." Surely, if I speak slowly and loudly they'll get a gist of what I'm saying "BUT. WE'RE. FINE. WHERE. WE. ARE," I yell. They look at me as if I'm deranged, and then at each other, bewildered.

"You don't understand," Panos says excitedly. He puts his hands on my shoulders and turns me towards the horizon. "This is their property."

Acres and acres of land stretch before us.

"You mean....." My hand flies to my mouth.

"Yep! My grandparents are modest people. They like the simple life, but they own it all. The land, the olive groves, the vines. They said they built it up over the years for my late father and now…they want to give it to us as a wedding present!"

"Panos." I say astounded, holding my chest. "All this must be worth thousands of pounds!"

"Millions," I hear him say as I slip into unconsciousness.

A PASSIONATE CRIME

I didn't mean to hurt him. Not like this. This wasn't supposed to happen, wasn't part of the plan. I look down at him. My husband of six years, face down, blood everywhere.

"Madam," says the room attendant, hovering over Rob's body, eyes shining with fear, "we'll have to call the police." I stare at him, wordless. My heart pounding so hard, I fear it'll rupture through my chest.

A crowd has assembled outside our room, their voices sear through me. I cover my mouth. What've I done?

Everything was fine earlier. Rob had gone off to do a bit of sightseeing while I returned to our luxury hotel room. It was a hot, sticky afternoon. I needed to have a shower, freshen up. Two hours later, he strolled in, buzzing and smelling of booze. I hated it when he'd had one too many. He became erratic, needy. He snuck up behind me as I stared out of the window at the Castle.

"Rob…" I pulled away, "you startled me."

"Sorry," he said, smiling. "But, guess what I've been doing all afternoon?" Apart from drinking the brewery dry, I wanted to say, but didn't. I didn't want him to kick off. I needed to keep things calm between us for when I told him that I wanted a divorce. I wasn't going to walk away from this marriage with nothing.

He opened the red leatherette box in his hand to reveal the Celtic ring we'd seen earlier, and my heart sank. "I got the assistant to alter yours, it should fit perfectly now." He took my hand but I snatched it away.

"I told you I didn't want one. I've got lots of rings."

"But it's a Soul Mate ring," he said, sounding hurt. He was trying hard, but it was too late. Surely, he could see that our marriage was dead. Even he couldn't be that arrogant.

"We need to talk, Rob." My voice was firm, methodical.

"I thought that's what we were doing." He took my hand again and slid the ring on my finger, then began opening wardrobes, assembling clothes, all the while telling me about our evening plans.

As he rambled on, I sank into a brown leather armchair, depleted, and focused on a brass sculpture of an eagle on the sideboard. Its long, sharp beak, like a four-inch dagger, its beady eyes - chilling. I held my chin in my hand, staring at the unusual ornament in a daze, regretting this overnight stay by the second. I'd only agreed to leave Lily, our five-year-old daughter, with my sister for a sleepover to ask Rob for a divorce. I was hoping that the time alone would help me break the news to him, soften the blow. But he wasn't making this easy.

"And then I thought we could...." His voice again.

"Rob, please. Stop!" I got to my feet and studied my reflection in the large, oblong mirror above the wooden desk. It was time to come clean. I couldn't carry on playing happy families. I smoothed down my hair and faced him. "This isn't working out. You know that, don't you?"

"Oh?" He frowned, grabbed the remote control and lunged onto the bed. "I thought you were enjoying it. We haven't been away on our own since Lily was born." He switched the TV on and started flicking though the channels.

"No, not this." I looked around the room, twirling the soul mate ring around my finger as he settled down with a sports channel, completely unperturbed. "This!" I yanked it off, almost tearing my finger with it, and tossed it onto the bed next to him.

His face went pale. Finally, I had his attention. He switched the TV off. "Carrie, please, don't," he gulped, as if he knew what was coming.

"Come on, Rob. Don't make this difficult."

"But, I love you." He stood up, hands limply on hips.

I grabbed my overnight bag. "You don't, you can't. I can't cope with your bachelor lifestyle anymore. It isn't a wife you want. It's a cleaner, a nanny, a psychotherapist. I've had enough. " As I zipped my bag I felt his hand on my wrist.

"You're not leaving me," he said sternly. "I won't let you. Think of our daughter, our lovely home." I looked at his fingers curled around my wrist, then gazed up at him and he slowly released his grip. "I'll change." He swallowed hard, his Adam's apple bobbled in his throat. "I promise." Our eyes locked.

"It's too late, Rob," I said quietly. "I don't love you anymore." I looked away. "Jemma's told me everything."

His face went red as he leapt in front of me like a starfish, blocking my way. "We had sex twice, that's all. I swear on Lily's life. I told her I'd never leave you."

"What?" I felt a shot of acid dance in my stomach. "You've been sleeping with Jemma? Our neighbour Jemma?" I covered my lips with my cold, trembling fingers. Jemma had confided in me recently that whenever Lily and I went to see my parents in Devon, he'd be out all night. Sometimes not coming home at all. I never thought for one moment that....

He gave me a gormless smile. "She invited me round for dinner a few times," he said nervously, "while you were visiting your folks. I was lonely. I hate coming home to an empty house, you know that."

That was it. The last straw. "How could you, Rob?"

"Please, just let me just explain."

But I was furious – hurt – humiliated. "Get out of my way." I pushed past him.

"There's someone else, isn't there?" he shouted. I stopped dead at the door. My back to him.

"Rob, I want a divorce," I said tightly, not looking round. "I'm sorry." Then as I wrenched the door open, I came face to face with the room assistant, white towels stacked in her arms.

"Madam," she cried. We both dived out of the way as Rob flew between us. I looked down at him, horrified, the brass eagle clutched in his bleeding hand.

I watch him now as he stirs. "Sir," says the room attendant, "Shall I call an ambulance?" Rob staggers to his feet, blood on the floor, his shirt.

"I'm fine," he hisses, pushing past me. "And you lot can get lost. Show's over." He calls out to the astounded crowd.

"Madam?" the attendant's voice again.

"No, he seems okay," I say. "I'm sorry about the mess and disturbance." I smile and she nods kindly.

"Do you want me to call the police?" she whispers. I look round at Rob. He's sitting on the edge of the bed, cradling his injured hand, sobbing quietly like a lost little boy.

"No, there's no need. It was just a fight between us. Please charge our card for any damages."

"Are you sure, Madam?" Her blue eyes are pleading with mine. I can see that she thinks I'm a victim of domestic violence but she's wrong. Rob, with all his faults, has never laid a finger on me.

"Yes," I say quietly, "I'm sure. It's over now."

THE CLIENT

My last client is five minutes late. I chew the top of my pen as I study her name on my list, *Leana Andrews*. I haven't seen her before but she sounded quite desperate on the phone this morning.

"I'm afraid that I'm fully booked today," I told her, flicking through my diary. "But I can see you early next week."

"Please," she begged, "I can't wait that long, I don't mind paying extra."

I don't know why I agreed to squeeze her in after my last appointment. Perhaps it was the urgency in her voice. People do such drastic things when they're desperate, don't they, and I didn't want to feel responsible for her actions. I glance at my watch and recall Mark's warning over breakfast.

"Please be home on time tonight, Sam. Ellis has really splashed out on this work do and he's a stickler for punctuality. I don't want to get into his bad books, not with this promotion up for grabs." His lips brushed mine as he secured the knot in his tie, and who said that men couldn't multitask?

"Would I let my gorgeous husband down?" I teased. And with a raised eyebrow he told me that I'd better not. He knows me too well.

I look at my watch again. She's late. I can't wait any longer, Mark will be furious. But just as I turn the computer off, a young woman bursts through the door, drenched from the rain. Her blonde hair clinging to her neck and shoulders, her eyes smeared with running mascara.

"I'm so sorry I'm late," she quivers, "I've had such a rough day and…." I tell her not to worry, take her jacket and offer her a towel to dry off.

Once she's comfortably sitting on the leather chair, we begin.

"What can I do for you?" I smile.

Half an hour later Leana appears relaxed as she sips a cup of herbal tea and tells me all about her day. I always keep chamomile tea for clients who need calming, as well as a box of three-ply tissues. And I listen with sympathy, as always. *'You're just so easy to talk to,'* one client had said recently, *'and you always make me feel so good about myself.'* While another confided, *'I feel like I can trust you implicitly. I always walk out of here feeling so confident. I owe you so much.'*

Of course, it's comments like these that keep me so dedicated to my job. I turn my attention back to Leana.

"I've got this friend," she begins. I've heard this opening line so many times before with new clients. "She's only just found out that she's pregnant," she says, shuffling in her seat.

"Oh, that's nice," I offer, but the look on her face tells me that she isn't too pleased about it. "Is that a problem?"

"Maybe. Her husband doesn't want kids. Ever."

I smile softly and tell her that he may come round to the idea once he gets used to it. A lot of men do.

"Yes, but there's more." She bites her lower lip, "I'm not sure it's his." I keep a straight face. I'm not here to pass judgment on people.

"That might be a bit tricky," I say, "but I'm sure that your *friend* will be able to sort it out with him."

"Sort it out with him?" She looks mortified. "I'm not telling him." I manage to keep my composure. "Why should I?" she says indignantly, and then blushes as she becomes aware of her unwitting confession. "Oh well," she sighs, "It's not as if I know you, or that I'll ever see you again." Hmm…a one-off visit, I'd better make sure I make a lasting impression.

Leana speaks of her husband's frequent business trips abroad with sadness, tells me how miserable she feels and how she has needs too. "Surely you'd understand that?" she says, holding my gaze. I don't answer. This isn't about me. "Anyway," she huffs, "this baby deserves the best that life can offer." She rubs her non-existent bump affectionately, "There's a good chance that it's his and it's not as if he's short of money, if you know what I mean?"

It's 9 pm and the party's in full swing. I didn't have a chance to shower or change and I now stick out like a sore thumb amongst all these glamorous looking WAGS. I grunt, feeling frumpy and awkward and head for the luxurious looking buffet, surely I'll find something indulging there to comfort me.

"Didn't think I'd see you again," says a voice as I bite into a canapé. Leana is by my side looking every inch the fashionista in a perfectly styled beehive. "Small world," she says.

"Yes, erm.." It's not like me to be lost for words. "Do *you* work for Ellis', then?" I manage.

"No, my husband's worked for them for years," she says, studying her nails. "Anyway, listen," she hisses, her mouth inches from my ear, "you'd better not say anything about today, client confidentiality and all. I swear I'll have you for slander if any of what we said gets out." What happened to that desperate, vulnerable young thing I saw this afternoon? I take a sip from my wine glass and assure her that I won't. That I'm a professional. That I'd never break client confidentiality.

"Are you all right, Sam?" Mark refills my glass, "you look pale."

"That blonde girl over there, smooching with that man, do you know them?"

Mark looks at Leana and her husband swaying provocatively on the dance floor. Leana clocks us and narrows her eyes.

"Oh, yeah, Dan the man and his new missus," says Mark, hovering over the buffet table.

"Why do you call him that?" I whisper, linking my arm through his.

"He's a bit of a lady's man, that's all, renowned for his active business trips," he winks. "This is wife number three." He bites into a pastry hungrily. Anyone would think I didn't feed him.

"Any kids?" I quiz.

"You must be joking," he grins, "he's had the snip."

"Oh." I take a step back as a mixture of sadness and relief washes over me.

"Why the sudden interest in Dan, you don't fancy him do you?"

"Er...hello. I am a married woman, you know." I elbow him lightly on the arm. "I had his wife in this afternoon."

"Riiight." He looks at her, lips turned downwards, nodding approvingly. "Great job, the works?"

"Nah, just a wash and style." I take a sip of my cool, crisp wine, "And let's just say that she may soon be joining Dan the man's ex's club."

Heavenly Scent

"I wish I could do that," says a voice behind me. I stop in mid- track and look back up the steps.

"Excuse me?" I ask with a small smile. I'm running late but if she needs any help...

"Run down the stairs." The elderly lady waves a finger, "The way you're doing." I watch hesitantly as she takes one slow step at a time, her leather-gloved hand holding onto the railing for support. "Only you don't think old age will ever happen to you."

"Oh dear," I offer politely, "what can you do?" I edge away and hurry down the stairs. I close my eyes in disbelief as the 1830 whisks away on the tracks. I look up at the timetable display, '*Next train seventeen minutes.*'

Well, that's it now. By the time I get home, they'll be half way down the motorway. And is anyone going to believe what a day I've had? No chance. Mind you, who could blame them for thinking I didn't bother turning up to see them off after last night's fiasco of a farewell dinner?

"Why can't you just be happy for me?" said Natalie, my daughter, through trembling lips.

"Because you're making a big mistake, that's why," I replied, taking a sip of wine angrily. "You barely know each other!" Okay, maybe I was a bit harsh but how would you react if your nineteen-year-old daughter suddenly dumped everything for a life in Santorini with her Greek boyfriend of three months?

"What on earth are you talking about?" Natalie retorted, "Stelios and I are in love, aren't we, babe?" Stelios avoided my gaze as he put a protective arm around my daughter.

"Your Mamma needs time, isn't it, Linda?"

"Time!" Natalie pushed him away and Stelios gave me a look depicting, 'I tried'. But I didn't need his support. I knew how to handle my own daughter.

"She doesn't think you're good enough for me?" Natalie snapped.

But she'd got it all wrong. I quite liked Stelios. With his good looks and charm, he was every inch an Adonis. But she's got a life here. Family and friends who love her. A University degree to finish. Surely, she couldn't chuck it all in for a holiday romance.

"Girls, girls, let's just calm down and talk this through like adults." Joe stood up stretching his arms wide across the table, as if refereeing a wrestling match.

"Oh, at last, my husband has something to say." I threw my napkin onto the table and folded my arms.

"Don't take this out on Daddy. At least he cares enough to understand." Natalie and her father have always had a special bond. Joe always spoilt her rotten while I took on the role of disciplinarian. But it didn't mean I loved her any less.

"Come on, Stelios." Her chair scrapped loudly against the parquet, "I need some air." I stood up too.

"But, Natalie, why can't you both live here until…" I curled my hand around her arm gently but she shrugged me off furiously. I couldn't believe it. What was happening to our family? We used to be so close before Stelios came along.

"You might as well sit down, dear." The elderly lady pats the empty seat besides her and with a thin smile I do as I'm told.

She smells of jasmine. That takes me back a few years. I close my eyes briefly. I'm sitting in front of an open fire, snuggled in the safety of my Nan's arms.

"Hard day at work, love?" says the old lady, her voice cutting into my daydream. Goodness, the dark puffy circles under my eyes must look worse than I thought.

"Something like that." I look up at the flashing display screen. "Oh, grrreat," I say through gritted teeth, raking my fingers through my hair angrily.

"What does it say, dear?" She squints at the display.

"Further delays expected."

She gives me a sympathetic smile. "Don't worry, love. Why don't you call home and let them know you're running late?" When I tell her that my phone battery is flat, her hand disappears into her handbag. "Here," she offers, "you can use mine. Don't worry, it's free." She smiles at my expression, "What's an old woman like me doing with an iPhone?"

"No…I…" But before I can finish she gives me a rundown of how her daughter bought it for her for emergencies.

"She works very hard, you know," she says proudly with a nod, "I don't get to see her much but she's always in my thoughts."

"Oh," I say, intrigued, "why not?"

"She works in Paris." She stares into the distance. "But visits regularly," she adds quickly, "you know, to spend time with me and see her friends and that."

"Don't you miss her?"

She tells me she does, painfully. "But it's what she wants," she shrugs. "I can't stand in the way of her happiness."

I look down into the darkness of the tracks. She can't love her as much as I do Natalie. They can't be as close. I can't bear the thought of being parted from her.

Then as if the old lady can read my mind, she says, "Every mother loves her child, dear. But there comes a time when you have to let go," she winks and gives my hand a light squeeze. "You've got to let them learn by their own mistakes, and remember that you were young and foolish once too." She takes a deep breath as she pulls her black Birkin handbag close to her chest. Another gift, I wonder, from her daughter. She must be doing really well. "That's my motto, anyway."

I search her grey eyes but her honest gaze doesn't flinch. Suddenly I feel like I've known her forever and everything seems to make sense.

I look at my watch thoughtfully. If I take a taxi, I might just catch them. I'll explain how sorry I am, that although it isn't what I want I will try to understand, try to accept Natalie's decision. I'll tell her that her happiness comes before mine. That would make everything right between us again, I'm sure of it. I turn to thank the elderly lady but she's gone. She must've slipped away while I was in deep thought.

The look of urgency on Natalie's face staring at me through the window tells me all is not well. But I'll put it right, they'll see. Once I've told them about my change of heart they'll be thrilled. But as my hand reaches for the garden gate the front door springs open and Natalie and Joe tumble out towards me.

"What's going on? You're suffocating me the pair of you."

"Thank goodness," says Joe, kissing my head repeatedly.

"Oh, Mum, I'm so sorry." Natalie throws her arms around me.

"What's happened?" I'm happy they're pleased to see me and obviously I've been forgiven, but this is a bit over the top.

"Haven't you heard, Linda?" I look at Joe, confused. Stelios is standing by the door, his face ashen.

"The train crash? The six-thirty from Victoria? It's been all over the news."

"What? I missed my usual train. I got sidetracked by an old dear and...."

"Well she must've been your guardian angel," Joe interrupts. And just at that moment, I swear I smell a hint of jasmine in the cold evening air.

TABLE MANNERS

I knew he was Italian from the very first moment I set eyes on him. He had those dark, penetrating eyes and that moody expression. I remember the way he looked at me as I approached the counter through long, luxurious, black eyelashes. When he spoke, in that husky accented voice of his, I wasn't disappointed.

"Ciao, Bella, what can I get ya?" Okay, it was a corny line but who was complaining? I ordered a mozzarella and tomato Panini and a large decaf, skinny Latte. "Come on," he teased, "you don't need a skinny Latte, you already a skinny lady." If only. I still couldn't get into my favourite pair of jeans, despite constant dieting. But Italians like their women curvy, don't they? So, I took it as a compliment with a sprinkling of humour from a very dishy Italian chef.

Six months later, I walk into the same café, wearing my favourite pair of skinny jeans with room to spare. But I don't need to place my order anymore. I just sit at 'my table' as Luigi endearingly calls it. And I wait while he prepares something low fat and delicious for me. Sometimes, when he's not too busy, he joins me at 'my table,' sips Espresso and tells me stories about his childhood in Sicily, and I listen in amazement. Luigi has this special gift, you see, he can make any woman feel like a princess, regardless of age, shape or size. Only, I'm short of one thing - a prince charming. But hopefully that's all about to change.

I'm feeling a bit jittery about taking Luigi home to meet mum. Who'd have thought that after all those dates, Luigi would be the one to fit the bill? Doubtless, she'll have her reservations, she always does, but he's the only one who passed '*the food test,*' you see, so she can't complain about that. Let me explain. Mum has this theory about eating habits.

"You can tell a lot about people by the way they eat their food, Lucy, all you have to do is learn how to read them," she said over Sunday lunch three weeks ago.

"What, you mean like tarot reading?" I teased, knowing that mum hated anything to do with the paranormal.

"Oh, don't be so ridiculous." She took a sip of wine, then fixed me with one of her looks and I knew I wasn't going to like what was coming next. "That speed dating thingy you're going on with Carole?" My eyes narrowed suspiciously. I was wondering when we'd get round to this. "It's a bit old fashioned, isn't it? I hope you're not going to date men old enough to be your father."

"Oh, mum, don't start." She's right, of course, speed dating is very 90s but it's an event set up by Carole's sister as a bit of a launch for her new bar in town. I could hardly refuse. Besides, it might be fun.

"Hmm…well, I'm just saying," she replied hastily, cutting into her roast chicken. "Anyhow, I was wondering if you'd do me a little favour."

"A favour? What kind?" I asked guardedly. Surely she didn't want to come with us now she was single again?

"Have dinner with each man who contacts you on your list, study their eating habits, then report back to me. I swear I'll pick out your prince charming for you." I let out a sigh of relief. And although I was a bit dubious, I agreed. What harm could it do? And it would give me a peaceful life.

Dinner date number one was a pompous bore and, to be honest, I couldn't wait to get rid of him. So I made my excuses before dessert and escaped.

"You're back early, was he that bad?" Mum asked sympathetically.

"Mum, he ate like a horse and bored me to tears," I said kicking off my shoes.

"Greed," said Mum, "not a good trait, cross him off the list."

And I was only too happy to. Dinner date number two went fairly well.

"Well, how did it go?" asked Mum eagerly the next day.

"Not bad, actually. He barely touched his food though, just fiddled around with his main course while playing footsy with me under the table."

"Oh, that's disgraceful," Mum retorted, "Dining out on a full stomach. Mean and sex mad. Ditch him!"

By dinner date number three I was tiring of it all and beginning to think that Mum was right, speed dating was a waste of time. I arrived late and there didn't seem to be anyone waiting for me outside the restaurant. Perhaps he'd been and gone. To be honest, I was half pleased. I folded my arms and leant forward on the sole of my foot, peering through the restaurant window. It looked smart, fine dining, for sure. At least he wasn't mean, albeit unreliable and impatient.

"You're late," came a voice from behind me. Startled, I spun round and there he was. My Prince Charming. All six foot two of him, his blue eyes shining against his tanned skin and black, vibrant hair. A smile swept over my face as my eyes fell onto his broad shoulders and well defined biceps veiled beneath an expensive looking blue cotton shirt.

"I'm Danny." He held out his hand, and when I took it he drew it to his mouth and softly brushed his luscious lips against my fingers, sending all kinds of sensations through me. Why couldn't I remember this fit man at the speed dating night? Mind you, chatting to over thirty men, with a three minute per man limit, under the influence of quite a few glasses of Prosecco might answer that.

Inside the restaurant we sat at a cosy table under an alcove. We dined on the finest food, sipped champagne and exchanged intimate glances. I was smitten, only the next day Mum wasn't impressed.

"Darling, if he left his favourite food on the plate till last then he's a procrastinator, too easy going. It'll be a job getting him down the aisle, I can tell you. Chuck him before it's too late."

I was disappointed, to say the least. But I carried on crossing the men off my list to see if mum really could pick out Mr. Perfect.

Dinner date number four cut his food into equal portions. Mum's analysis was 'fastidious and hell to live with.' Number five was even worse. He mashed most of his food up with the gravy.

"Yuk," said mum, "do you want to live with a slob for the rest of your life?" I was at the end of my tether and my list, for that matter. Then I secretly had dinner with Luigi but told mum he was number six on my list.

"So, you're saying that he ate his favourite bits first?"

"Yes, Mum, and I did ask him why."

"And what did he say?" she asked, excitedly.

"That he eats the best bits first in case he fills up on the rest of the food and misses out."

"Darling, he sounds perfect." She pressed one hand on her chest and stared into the distance, as if reading the last lines of a Shakespearean tragedy at a London theatre. "That means he seizes life, enjoys the moment. Bring him home for tea."

So here we are. Luigi sitting on mum's floral sofa looking as gorgeous as ever, his dark eyes shifting from me to mum. And Mum looking uncomfortable under his penetrating gaze.

"Well?" I whisper enthusiastically in the kitchen. "He's well buff, isn't he?"

"Buff? He's not a trophy, dear, although you do seem to be treating him like one."

"Oh Mum," I tap her lightly with a tea towel. "I mean isn't he good-looking?"

"Yes, darling, he's very 'buff'. But isn't he a bit….. old?" As I open my mouth to speak, Luigi's head appears around the door.

"Need any help, Mrs Bennet?"

"Ah, Luigi." Mum blushes. "No, you sit yourself down. We've got it all under..." But he's already taking the lasagne out of the oven. "Bellissimo, Mrs Bennet, this smells fantastico." He kisses his fingertips and shoots them out into the air like a star.

"And what is this for starter? Oysters!" he growls playfully.

Dinner is perfect. Luigi entertains us with his Sicilian stories, his arms waving around in the air expressively. I haven't seen mum enjoy herself this much in years.

"You know, Mrs Bennet."

"Oh, call me Linda, for God's sake." She pours more wine, a good sign.

"Linda, you did fantastic job bringing up Lucy." Mum and I shrug smugly and exchange glances. "And I'm so glad she says you need a man." Wine splutters from mum's mouth. I stare at Luigi, horrified.

"I beg your pardon?"

"Mum, this isn't how it seems," I lean over, mopping the spilled wine with my napkin.

"Che?" Luigi shrugs, palms open. "I say wrong thing?"

I glance at Luigi. "No, Luigi but…"

"Mrs…Linda, when Lucy had dinner with me last week and said, 'Luigi, you'd be a perfect match for my Mamma,' I was…how you say in English? Shock. But now I see you, Lucy was right, you are a bella donna." Mum looks at me wide-eyed and aghast while I try hard to stifle a giggle. I come clean. "Mum, Luigi's your blind date," I say flatly.

Okay, maybe it was a bit sneaky of me, but she's been so lonely since my dad left her for a younger woman. And poor Luigi, so much zest, so much passion, and widowed at the tender age of thirty-eight. Wasn't it a shame that two beautiful people should walk the path of life alone?

Soon we're all laughing, and Luigi stays for coffee and Tiramisu while I slip away quietly. I've a date with Danny at eight. No food theory is going to make me pass on a dish like him. Besides, I always save the best till last too.

NEVER LET YOU GO

"Mind if I sit here?" a voice says. I look up from my iPhone. I'm halfway through texting Jake, letting him know that I'm here and he's late. I'm feeling slightly anxious, actually. His text message earlier sounded quite serious - *Meet me at the park bench by the swings at 1pm – we need 2 talk. J x.*

I wonder if he wants to finish with me. I knew I shouldn't have sent him that midnight Whatsapp message saying *'I luv u.'* - what was I thinking? We've only been together three months.

The woman swerves her sleeping toddler in his buggy and locks the brake expertly with her foot, her free hand carefully wrapped around a Starbucks cup. I glance at my leather bag on the bench, she offers me a thin smile and I'm tempted to move it. But actually, I'd rather she didn't sit with me. I *really* need to talk to Jake - alone.

"I'm sorry but...." I begin, but she's already sitting down.

I go back to my text message *'Where r u?'* I harrumph in exasperation, my heart fluttering in my chest, then just as I'm about to press 'send' the woman yelps, "Ouch," then pulls a pharmacy bag from under her seat, "this yours?"

"Yes," I snatch it from her hastily. "It must've fallen out of my handbag." I stuff the packet back into my bag.

"Nice bag," she says. The aroma from her coffee cup whisks its way into my nostrils as she removes the lid, stirring my stomach. "Looks expensive," she takes a small sip. The foam has formed a thin moustache on her top lip, which I'm compulsively drawn to.

"Thanks." I say, pulling it towards my thigh. "It was a gift." From Jake, actually, but I don't need to tell her that.

"He's got good taste," she says, as if she can read my mind. She stares into the distance, blowing on her steaming coffee, and I look at her properly for the first time. She's a pretty brunette, about my age, with a roundish figure. I scan her fingers discreetly. She's not wearing a ring. I wonder if she's a single mum in need of adult company. She looks tired, worn out. I'm flushed with a mixture of sympathy and gratitude. It's not easy to find a catch like Jake. I know I'm very lucky.

"I wish I'd met you sooner," Jake had said, just the other day as we snuggled on my sofa in front of the T.V, with a bottle of wine and a DVD. Jake's divorced with two children that he sees every weekend. We agreed it's too soon for them to meet me, which means weekends are out, but we're coping. Besides, it won't be for long. He's told them all about me.

"I'd never have cheated on you," he said gently, "your ex-husband must've been a complete twat." He was right about that. Matthew was a player.

"We could still be happy," I offered. "We're only in our thirties. It's not too late to..."

He sighed deeply, covering my mouth gently with his fingers. "Always the optimist," he whispered, 'I'll never let you go. You know that, don't you?"

The lady on the bench gives me a gentle nudge.

"I've got one just like it." I furrow my brows. "The bag. Only mine's in black. My husband bought it for me on our anniversary last year." So I was wrong about her being a single mum, then. I wonder why she doesn't wear her ring. If it were me, I'd never take it off. "Don't know what he's going to buy me this year." She rests her hand over her tummy, "With number three on the way."

"Oh, I didn't notice," I lie, well, I can't tell her that I thought she was a bit overweight, can I? "Congratulations," I say, cheerily.

"Are you married? Kids?" She holds my gaze over her coffee cup.

"No," I smile, "Well, not yet.... " I falter. "I'm with someone new, so..."

"It's love, then, is it?" she says indignantly, pushing her long fringe off her face and tucking it behind her ear. Her bluntness startles me and I feel my cheeks tingle. "Sorry," she adds, "I can tell by the sparkle in your eyes. I'm a bit of a cynic when it comes to love." She grins but her smile doesn't quite reach her eyes. "Well, enjoy it while it lasts because it won't." Great, that's all I need today, a pessimist to rain on my parade. "That's what happens when you rush into marriage, like I did." She crushes the empty polystyrene cup in her hand and tosses it into the bin. I take it things aren't going too well for her at home, then.

Her words stamp heavily on my mind. I've only known Jake a short while. She's right. We shouldn't rush into anything, not after what we've both been through. I'll tell him that I'm sorry about the message last night. That it was the wine talking.

"This lovely little thing was an accident," she sighs, her voice cutting into my thoughts. Her hand disappears inside her bag. "Here." She holds her mobile phone under my nose. "A photo we took last week."

I smile as she points out her children snuggled against her.

"And my other-half," she groans. I look at the handsome man in the photo, his arm draped loosely over her shoulders, his palm protectively covering her slightly showing bump, his familiar lopsided grin tearing into my heart.

"Jake," I gasp, my hand flies to my mouth. "Oh my God."

My phone is still in my hand, hovering over the 'send' button. I press down on it hard. Seconds later a familiar tune buzzes in her hand.

"I don't believe this. What's going on? Who are you?" I struggle for breath. I feel faint, giddy.

"Who do you think I am?" she barks, looking at me as if I'm mad. "What a flipping cheek."

"But...but...you're divorced," I manage with a wobbly voice.

"The thing is," her voice is suddenly calm, firm, "we're still very married."

With clammy hands I call his office. He answers on the third ring.

"Jake, what's happened to your phone? I hold onto the bench armrest, trying to steady my quivering body.

"Sorry, Tess, I've been searching for it all morning. Did I leave it round yours?"

"No," I say sternly, "You didn't. Your wife has it. She's with me now." There's a dark silence.

"Tess," he pleads, "I...I can explain." I can hear the panic in his voice escalating. "It's not what you think. Is Sophie there? Put her on. Where are you? Tess? Tess? Are you still there? "

I end the call and look at Sophie sadly. I can't believe I've been the other woman, not after all I've been though.

"I'm so sorry," I say softly, standing up.

"Wait," her hand curls around my arm. "You really didn't know, did you?" I shake my head, giddy with disbelief. "Please." Her grip tightens, "Promise me you'll end the affair." I can't believe this. Why isn't she crying, screaming, shouting – anything but this!

"Don't you care?" I look at her aghast. A big tear spills from my eye and slides down my face.

"Well, of course I do." Her voice is thick with emotion, "But you're not the first." She looks away, "He always does this when I'm pregnant."

I close my eyes briefly. What a complete bastard. "Then why stay with him?"

"I've got two children and one on the way, how will I cope alone? And besides," her voice drops to a whisper, "I love him. I'll never let him go."

I grab my bag and fling it over my shoulder.

"It's over," I say, quietly. "You have my word."

And I walk into the afternoon, a single woman, grateful that I narrowly escaped another disastrous relationship with a man I hastily trusted.

MY GIRL

Max honked the car horn twice and waited.

"He's here," shouted Louise, yanking back the net curtain.

"Mum," Rosie exclaimed, peeking over her shoulder, "stop staring at him, it's rude." Rosie clipped on her left earring and climbed into her new stiletto shoes.

"You'll get blisters in those five-inch heels by the end of the evening," Louise grumbled, giving them a disapproving glance. "I suppose *he* bought them for you?"

"Er, hello? I am seventeen, you know. I can pick out my own clothes." Rosie knew that her mother meant well but sometimes she treated her like she was still five-years-old.

"Well, at least he spends his money on you, I suppose," Louise groaned, folding her arms. "Anyway, why doesn't he knock for you like a decent human being, instead of sitting outside in that flash car of his trying to impress the neighbours?"

"Because we all know what happened the last time he came in for a quick coffee, don't we, Mum?"

Rosie cringed at the thought of the row that erupted between the two of them a few weeks ago.

"Oh, so it's my fault now, is it?" Louise snapped, "Bringing you home drunk at your age."

"Oh, Mummmm. I only had, like, one small glass of wine with my food," Rosie complained, pulling her coat on, "you over-reacted, as per."

"You're still underage," Louise said defensively, "And you're still my daughter. It's my job to be concerned." She smiled, and then drew Rosie into her arms, savouring her scent. "Everything's changing so fast," she whispered into her hair, her voice muffled with emotion. "I remember when you used to cuddle up to me and your dad on the sofa, watching cartoons, like it was yesterday." Louise held her daughter at arm's length and looked into her blue eyes. "My girl, all grown up."

"We're still a family, Mum," Rosie said warmly, "It's gonna be all right, I promise."

"Oh, listen to me," Louise sniffed, regaining her composure. "Go on, have a lovely time, and make sure he brings you home at a decent hour."

Rosie closed the front door behind her and walked awkwardly towards the waiting car. These new designer shoes were proving to be a bit of a task. Perhaps her mum was right, after all, she thought, wishing she'd slipped on her usual pumps. Max waved from the car and smiled as she approached him.

"Hello, gorgeous," he said, dropping a kiss on her forehead, "I see Cruella is checking up on me again," he joked, gesturing towards the window. Rosie looked back just as the curtains twitched.

"Shush, you, she's not that bad," she said, fastening her seatbelt, "Anyway, I wish you could make an effort to get along, at least for my sake." She hated the fact that the two most important people in her life didn't see eye to eye, couldn't sort out their differences. But she also knew that they were just as stubborn as each other.

"Actually, Rosie." Max unbuttoned his jacket, stretched his arm over the steering wheel and faced her. A diamond encrusted cufflink sparkled at his wrist. Rosie hadn't seen him wearing cufflinks before. They suited him – gave him an upbeat, sophisticated edge. "I know how upset you are that your mum and I can't get along." He bit on his thumbnail, staring out of the window thoughtfully.

"But if you'd just apologise," Rosie said urgently, "I know she'll come round, and things can just…."

"Rosie," Max interrupted, then sighed loudly. "Look, I was going to tell you this over dinner, but I suppose now is as good a time as any." Rosie felt her stomach twist as she looked at Max's serious face, and she knew she wasn't going to like what was coming next.

"Go on," she said with a frown.

"Well, the thing is." He scratched his chin. "I've met someone else."

"What?" Rosie exploded, stunned. "You are joking me, right?" The shock shot through her like lightning. Her cheeks felt like they were on fire.

"It's nothing serious," Max added quickly. Rosie took a deep breath and tried to digest what Max had just confessed. Her mobile phone bleeped in her bag.

"Mum was right about you all along," she managed, swallowing back her tears. How could she have been so stupid? So naïve?

"No," Max blurted quickly. "There was never anyone else until now, I swear." Rosie's eye caught his cufflink again, and she stared at it thoughtfully.

"They're new," she said accusingly, "I suppose *she* bought them for you?"

"Come on, Rosie," Max pulled his sleeve over his shirt-cuff nervously, "you're almost an adult now. You do understand, don't you?"

"They make you look rubbish," she cried angrily, wanting to hurt him back.

Max bit down on his lips, shaking his head. "Sweetheart, you've always known the score. I've never lied to you," he said softly, placing a warm hand over hers. "Look, we are okay, aren't we?"

But in one single moment, everything had changed. All her hopes and expectations – shattered. Her mobile bleeped again.

"Better get this, Dad," she said, glad of the distraction. Max sighed heavily as he turned on the ignition, while Rosie answered her phone, blinking back the tears and finally accepting that her parents' marriage was over for good.

DATE ESCAPE

I've fancied Mr Taylor for ages - from that very first moment I met him at parents' evening when Layla was just ten. Who'd have thought that five years on I'd be sitting opposite him in a pizzeria on a date?

"What're you going to have, Hannah?" he asks, chin in hand, musing at the menu.

I twist my lips thoughtfully as my mobile phone flutters on the table with a new message. It's probably Denise, my neighbour and fellow divorcee, wanting to know if I need her on stand-by.

We've got this deal, you see, it's called the First Date Escape, for when things don't quite go according to plan. All I have to do is text her and she'll call immediately with a bogus emergency so that I can make my excuses and leave.

Denise and I have had our share of calamitous dates arranged on *dateymatey.com*, from dodgy photos to fabricated personalities. The last straw came when one bloke suggested moving closer to where I lived. I had to change my telephone number and email to get away from him. Then just as I was about to close my account David Taylor's gorgeous face appeared on my screen.

I thought my dreams had come true when he remembered me and asked to meet-up. But now that I'm here, I'm not so sure.

"I think I might just have a Margherita," I reply, one hand holding the menu, the other checking my phone. I was right. It's Denise.

I text hurriedly - *Too soon. He's ok but ..*

"A Margherita?" David yells, and I almost drop the phone from my hand. I don't suppose he can leave his teacher persona in the classroom. "Why don't you try something a bit more adventurous?" A roar of laughter tears across the room and he winces. Clearly, he doesn't enjoy noisy places, whereas I love a good, rowdy crowd. "Go on," he insists, "live a little."

"Hmm…" I twiddle with my heart pendant as my phone buzzes with another message. "But I like cheese and tomato. I'm a bit of a traditionalist. Boring, I know."

He returns his attention back to the menu with a baffled expression as I retrieve my message. It's Layla, asking how the date's going.

I reply quickly, aware of his exasperated gaze. - *So far, so good, but...*

"A Margherita it is, then," David says as a stunning waitress appears at his side.

The evening goes fairly well. He tells me how fascinated he was that fate brought us together via *dateymatey.com*. He's still teaching but at a school nearer home. Has never married and isn't in a rush to go down the aisle.

"What, never?" I exclaim.

"Divorce statistics are pretty high," he says gravely.

"Oh, I agree," I say. "But never say never. I mean, I am only thirty-five. It's not too late to...."

"You don't want any more kids though, do you?" he cuts in, "not at your age." He slices into his pizza. "Not that you look that old." I gaze at him, aghast, wordless.

I take a swig from my third glass of wine, angrily. So far I've been insulted, ignored and shouted at. I think it's about time Denise got that call.

Don't get me wrong, David's gorgeous and quite good company, but do I really want to be with a man who's blunt to the point of rudeness, who yells if he's not got my full attention, who gives me patronising glares every time I touch my phone? And to top it all, he's made it quite clear that he's not interested in marriage and family. I don't think he's for me.

I reach for my phone as it tinkles with another alert. "Those things can be a menace." He nods towards my phone. "I only use mine for calls, except for when we texted earlier, that is. I always respond."

"Really? I don't think I could function without mine."

"I'd noticed," he says wryly, patting his lips with his napkin. Right. That's it. I open my mouth to speak. "Coffee?" he offers firmly, "I'll order some at the bar while I go to the little boys' room." And before I can answer he's sashaying across the bustling restaurant, long limbs swaying almost in time to the loud background music.

Once he's out of sight. I grab my phone and start jabbing at the keyboard. I've got to act quickly. Men don't take long in the loo.

Denise! Help. Driving me nuts. Shouty voice. Told me I'm too old at 35. Gorgeous but rude! Hurry up!

I press send, drop the phone onto the table, then lean back in my seat. A sigh of relief slithers from my lips as I await my escape call.

He's back, sitting in front of me, fingers entwined, face grave. "Have you had a disappointing evening?"

"What?" My phone starts ringing. Oh goodness, it must be Denise. I should pick up. "Of course not," I lie.

"It's just that you seem..." he shrugs. "I thought we'd hit it off and.....look, do you want to get that?" he says with a loud sigh.

"Nah," I wave a hand, "it's probably just PPI."

"But it might be important."

As I answer my phone, he takes his from his pocket and presses it to his ear.

"Hello," I murmur.

"Hello," he says, his eyes not leaving mine. I look at him in stunned silence. "I'm sorry you thought I shouted at you. I couldn't hear you. I've got a hearing aid in here." He points to his ear, "and it's not so good in noisy places. I thought you said you were forty-five."

"Oh no," I gulp. "I'm so sorry. I thought you didn't like me. And when you kept shouting I....I" I stutter. "But how..."

He ends the call, then scrolls through his messages. "You just sent me this." He shows me the text meant for Denise. "You really ought to be more careful in the future."

My hand flies to my mouth, shame sluicing through me. "I'm so, so sorry, David," I mutter, "I've been a complete first date nightmare." I slip my mobile phone into my bag and zip it firmly. "I know it's too much to ask, but can we please start again?"

OPEN WIDE

I'm having one of *those* days. You know the type, where everything seems to go wrong. In the last forty-eight hours I've managed to lose a boyfriend and a filling in my tooth. I twirl my tongue over the cavity and grunt, and then just as I think things couldn't possibly get any worse a voice says,

"Excuse me?" I look up at a frazzled looking woman. "Could you save that seat for me please?" she gasps, one hand on her ample chest, the other clutching several shopping bags.

"That one?" I look at the empty seat at the table next to mine. "Yes," I say instinctively. The woman beams at me, then hurries off to the coffee bar. I stir my coffee thoughtfully. Why did I agree to such an inane request? What will I say if someone else comes along? *"Sorry but you can't sit there because I'm saving it for a stranger who's joined the bottom of that long queue.'* Perhaps Connor was right - I am a bit of a pushover.

I check my iPhone for messages in case he's texted to beg forgiveness. He hasn't. I chew the inside of my lip. Maybe I should call him? After all, I was the one who did the dumping. I start scrolling through my contacts list. I'll give Carrie a quick call at the office first in case he's called there in my absence.

"No," she says in exasperation, "and you're well rid of him if you ask me." Only I wasn't asking, was I? "Besides," she lowers her voice to a whisper, "I shouldn't really be telling you this, Tom will kill me if he knew, but we've set up another blind date for you." Oh please, give me strength, not another blind date. "His name is Ambrose," Ambrose? "And don't be put off by his name," she protests quickly, as if she could read my mind. "I've told him all about you and…well you'll find out soon enough." For heaven's sake, not another one of Tom's ex-uni friends to bore me into a coma.

"Anyway," she adds hastily, "aren't you supposed to be at the dentist?" I can just imagine her narrowing her green eyes. I don't answer. "Cathy, you'd better turn up! Dr Reeves squeezed you in as a favour."

How could I forget? She's been reminding me all morning. But I'm terrified of dentists. Besides, there's nothing seriously wrong with my tooth, apart from that niggling pain around the cavity. A couple of strong painkillers will sort that out in a jiffy.

"I'm on my way there now," I lie, "call me if Connor rings." She huffily agrees, then hangs up abruptly.

Why do I always fall for the bad boys? I knew that Connor was a player from the start but convinced myself that I'd be the one to change him, that if only he met the right woman…. I sigh deeply.

"Oooh, thanks for that, love," the woman's back with a steaming cup of tea. "I'm meeting my son for lunch soon," she says, cosying down in the seat next to mine.

"Hmm," I murmur, my thumb hovering over Connor's phone number.

"What's up with your face, dear?" She takes a small sip from her cup then presses her ruby lips together. Goodness, I must look worse than I feel.

I look up briefly and smile, "Overworked and underpaid."

She laughs, then adds, "No, I mean all that swelling." She gesticulates around her own mouth as an example.

"What?" My hand shoots to my mouth as I leap to my feet. I stare at my reflection in the mirror behind our seats in horror. "Oh my goodness," I say. I look like I'm auditioning for the lead part in The Godfather.

"You need a dentist, love." She takes another sip of tea. "Dr. Reeves on Hanover Square is…." But before she can finish I grab my bag and the next thing I know I'm sitting in the Dental Surgery.

I take a magazine from the neat pile on the table and thumb through it nervously. Deep breaths, Cathy, I tell myself, deep breaths.

"Miss Price?" I glance up at a handsome face, and for a brief moment everything seems hazy. This can't be him? *'Gentle, Mature, receding, you know the type.'* Carrie had said when I asked her what he was like.

"Dr. Reeves." He extends a muscular arm. Oh my goodness, I can't believe it. "Will you come this way please?" I trot behind him. This can't be happening to me, not today.

"Just relax, Miss Price." I recline onto the leather chair rigidly. "When did you last have a check-up?" He shines the light onto my face and suddenly I feel like I'm under criminal investigation.

"Oh, er…about six months ago…?" I lie. It's been at least four years.

"Open wide for me please." I hold my breath in an effort to curb any bad fumes from drifting to his nostrils.

"Bit more than six months, Miss Price," he says with a wide grin, revealing a perfect set of celebrity white teeth, which make mine look like

I've been living in a tree for the last thirty-four years.

"Rinse please, and I'll have a look at that cavity."

I swish the pinkish liquid around in my mouth. The trouble is, when I feel nervous I get the giggles.

"So, how long have you known Carrie?" I say, trying to stifle a laugh. He looks uncomfortable and blinks a few of times. Surely, they didn't. She couldn't have! The little minx.

"Tom and I were student pals," he says finally, with two spurts from the air compressor.

I wriggle around on the chair in agony, my nails digging into the armrests, my leg hanging off the edge of the seat as the whir of the drill bounces off the walls.

Then suddenly I let out a little yelp. "I'm sorry," he says softly, "did I hurt you?" And for a brief moment our eyes lock. "Just one last look and we'll be done for today."

"Rinse please." I lean over the small white basin, saliva dribbling down my chin. I want to die. "So..." He stuffs cotton wool between my lip and gum, pushes a vacuum pump under my tongue then starts probing, "have *you* known Tom and Carrie long?" Great, the first bit of chat-up and I have half the clinic's dental equipment hanging out of my mouth. I mumble something completely incoherent.

"All done, Miss Price," he says brightly. "You've got an abscessed tooth. I want you to take some antibiotics then come back and see me in a week." A week? Another visit? Hmm...I think I could manage that in his capable hands. He leads me out to the foyer and asks the receptionist to book me in.

"Ah, you found it, then, love." I spin round. I'm face to face with the lady from the cafe.

"Hello, Mum," says Dr. Reeves, pulling her into his arms. "Do you two know each other?"

"Yes, Ambrose." Ambrose? Oh. My. God. Carrie, how deliciously clever of you. "This lovely young lady saved a seat for me in the café earlier. You don't get kind people like that anymore, Ambrose, love. My feet were aching."

They grin at each other and then at me, appreciatively. I give them small nod and a little modest smile, glad of my earlier good deed, and, of course, grateful to my good, albeit sneaky, friend Carrie.

No Way Back

Jake swishes Ollie back and forth in his pram. We're at our local park, gazing into the distance, cup of Starbucks in hand. To any onlooker we'd look like the perfect family, only we're not. Far from it, in fact.

I take a sip from my cup then place it next to me on the bench, gathering the lapels of my coat under my chin. It's turned cold, frosty. "Is he warm enough?" I ask, leaning forward and tucking Ollie in.

"Yes, he's fine," Jake says, "Don't worry."

"I can't stay long." I glance at my watch quickly, "We're short staffed at the nursery today." I pull the blanket close to Ollie's' face, feeling Jake's eyes on me all the while. "Babies can pick up all sorts of things these days, you can't be too careful."

Jake's a great dad but I know how blasé he can be about important things. Important things like our marriage, for instance.

"Sarah," he says quietly, "Leave him, he's fine." He gesticulates at Ollie with his coffee cup, "Stop fussing."

"Did you layer him up before you left the house?" I'm babbling, I know, but I can't help myself.

"Sarah, for heaven's sake." He puts his coffee cup on the floor then faces me. "Don't leave me." He takes my hands in his, squeezing my wedding band. "I love you." His green eyes search mine. "And I know you still love me too. I can see it in your eyes."

"You lied to me, Jake," I say, my voice cracking. "How can I ever trust you again?"

He looks away, agitated, his hand clenched into a loose fist. "I know. I should've told you, but it was over between us long ago."

"Only it wasn't completely over, Jake, was it?"

He huffs and looks away. "She was a mistake."

"So, that makes it all right, then, does it?" I ask, my anger returning.

"Well, why not? I married you, didn't I? We're a family now. You and I."

I glance down at Ollie. He's woken up and is smiling at me, his little legs kicking the blanket off his tiny body. I shake my head at Jake, wordless.

I found out about his secret eighteen months into our marriage. She turned up unannounced on our doorstep while I was cooking our evening meal, looking like she hadn't slept in weeks. "Is your husband in?" she demanded, gazing over my shoulder, her eyes darting around our narrow hallway.

"I'm sorry," I said with a smile, pushing wisps of hair off my flour speckled face with my wrist. "Who shall I say is calling?"

"I need to see him. Now," she snapped. And before I could stop her she barged past me and began scouting around the rooms. Ollie, sensing the commotion, started wailing as I chased after her.

"Excuse me," I yelled, you can't just come barging into my home. Who the hell are you, anyway?" And then she was face to face with Jake in the living room. I'll never forget his face. He looked like he'd seen a ghost.

"Claudia," he gasped, "What are you doing here? How did you find me?"

"What?" I screeched incredulously, causing Ollie to cry louder, "you know her?"

"Sarah, please, this isn't what you think. Claudia." He moved towards her and with his hands on her shoulders manhandled her into the hallway. "You need to leave. Now! I need to speak to my wife."

But she was having none of it. "I'm not going anywhere until I get what I came for," she yelled, shrugging him off furiously. "No more happy families for you Mr. Perfect." She eyed me up and down, chest heaving, face red. "She needs to know the truth about her loving husband." And in one instant my whole world was torn apart.

"Please, Sarah," Jake's voice again. "Don't do this. We're stronger than that, you and I. We'll grow old together. Two old fogies sitting on a bench in Brighton eating fish and chips, that's what we said, remember?"

My eyes fill with tears. He leans forward, brushing my long blonde fringe off my face, gazing at me tenderly. And for one brief second, I forget everything and lean towards him until Ollie's cries tear between us like a guillotine.

I pull away, "He needs a feed," I say hurriedly, "did you bring anything with you?"

Jake quietens Ollie with a dummy. "Just say you'll think about it, Sarah. I don't want to move out. I'll do us a nice dinner tonight from scratch, yeah?" he says excitedly, "and we can talk properly then. Just give me this one chance to explain, please."

I look at Jake and then at Ollie and my heart twists. He looks so much like his dad. "What about him?" I say gesturing at Ollie, swallowing back another tear.

"What about him?" He's swishing the pram back and forth.

"We can't pretend he doesn't exist." I take Ollie's little chubby hand in mine and smile down at him. "I don't want you to be an absent father," I say thoughtfully. "I'm sorry, Jake. There's no way back for us. I want you to pack your bags and leave. Tonight."

"Oh come on, Sarah, so many couples get through this....I."

I shake my head. "No, when it's cracked, it can never be the same again."

He looks at Ollie sadly. "But we could find a new normal in time, couldn't we?"

"I'm sorry, Jake. I've made my mind up."

He leans back, arms stretched across the bench and squints at the winter sunshine. "I wish I could turn back time," he says despondently. "If only I'd met you first. I'd never have gone with her. She's not even my type."

"Yes well, perhaps if you'd been honest with me from the start instead of...." I throw my hands up in the air then wipe my cold tears with my thumbs. "You can't just pretend a baby doesn't exist. What were you thinking?" Silence. "Anyway, it's too late for if onlys."

Jake takes a deep breath and exhales loudly. "I wish Ollie was ours, Sarah. Yours and mine. I wish you were his mum instead of Claudia."

"So do I." I say softly. "So do I."

THE ACCIDENT

Molly looks at me worriedly as I check my text messages on my mobile phone. "So, what is it that's so urgent, then?" I ask with a long sigh, slipping the phone back into my bag. "That can't wait until tonight?" I glance up at the wall clock behind her. "I've got to get to work soon. And shouldn't you be at uni?"

"I rang in sick. Oh, don't look at me like that, Mother. I am ill." Now it's my turn to look worried. "Well, sort of." She glances away, secures a lose strand of hair behind her ear, then starts twisting it around her index finger. She always does this when she's troubled, always has, ever since she was a little girl.

"Molly," I say tentatively. I reach for her hand across the table, her fingers are cold. "If there's anything that's worrying you? You know you can talk to me, don't you?"

Molly and I have always had a good relationship. She always comes to me with her problems and I always help her sort them. We're a team. Friends as well as mother and daughter.

"Oh, Mum." She looks up at me desperately, tears brimming at her eyes, "It's all such a mess." And before I can say anything else, she slumps over the table and dissolves into a fit of tears.

"Come on, love, you're scaring me now," I say anxiously, my arm around her. "Are you sick?" She shakes her head and I feel the knot in my stomach dissipate. She stops crying. I dab her sodden face softly with a tissue. "Look, I'll call the office." I reach for my handbag. "Tell them I've had an emergency. We can spend the day together, how's that?"

"No," she insists, pushing my arm away. "It's okay. I'll be fine."

Molly takes a deep breath as I return to my seat opposite her. "Has this got anything to do with what was worrying you a few weeks ago?"

She nods furiously, then reaches inside her cardigan pocket and slides a small plastic bag towards me. "Open it," she says with a shaky voice.

I gasp at the long plastic tube in my hand, staring at the two blue lines through a mist of shock.

I close my eyes briefly as I regain my equilibrium. "Oh, Molly," I say as fresh tears spring to her eyes. "Look, don't panic," I curl my hand around her forearm. "We can work this out. Together."

"Work it out?" she asks crossly, "I don't think so." She shakes her head, then blows her nose nosily into a tissue. She's always been head strong, my Molly, takes after her father. Always does as she pleases. She was an A-grade student from the onset, had the lead role in all the school plays in Junior.

She's organised, diligent, fiery - a list maker, a planner. This is a shock to her system. But she'll come round, she always does.

"Everything's ruined now," she sobs, "University, travelling. The lot. It's over." She holds her head in her hands.

"Oh, I don't know about that," I offer, "lots of people return to education later on in life." She gives me a look across the table, the same one her father gives me when he wants me to shut up. "And as for travelling...."

"Oh, Mum, stop trying to make me feel better about this. Who goes backpacking with a baby?" She sighs deeply as she gazes out of the window at three magpies that've perched on the windowsill. It's turned cold and grey, a bit like my daughter's mood. "Nineteen is no age to be a mother," she says softly, breaking the silence.

"I was only twenty when I had you," I say smoothly.

She waves a hand, tears again. "It was different back in the day."

"None taken," I say indignantly. "I'm not that old, you know."

"Oh, you know what I mean." She stares into her lap, then proceeds to tear a tissue to shreds. "This wasn't part of the plan."

I smile. "You were an accident, and you're the best thing that's ever happened to me." She looks shocked and I realise that I've never told her this before. "Anyway, I still went to college, got a good job at your old school."

"I know, I know." She covers her face with her hands and takes a deep, heartfelt breath.

"What does Tony think?" I ask. Molly gives me another one of her looks. "Please tell me that you've told him?"

"I'll tell him tonight," she snaps quickly, not looking at me. "I need to get my head around it first."

"Does anyone else know?" I say in a high voice, which sounds almost like a squeak. I can't believe she's kept this from Tony. He has a right to know.

"Just a couple of my mates from uni."

"What does Cindy think?"

"Oh, she's over the moon." She throws her hands up in the air, "Excited! She's no idea how hard it is to bring up a child. You know Cindy, head strong," she sighs.

"Hmm," I say wryly, 'reminds me of someone I know." She looks up at me briefly, a small smile at her lips. I think she's coming around already.

"Well." I get to my feet and shoulder my bag, "You're going to have to come to terms with it,

Molly. It's happened now, and by the sounds of it there's no going back."

"I know mum, you're right, as always. Thanks for the pep talk." She pulls me into her arms and I take in her signature scent. "I'd better get back to uni." We disentangle. "I said I'd do a half day shift, they're short staffed as it is."

"That's my girl." I reach out and kiss her on both cheeks. "And congratulations, you're going to make a lovely grandmother."

THE VISITOR

I take a magazine from the pile on Ivy's bedside table as a strong, heady scent whisks its way into my nostrils and I sneeze twice. I dab at my nose with a crumpled tissue, throwing a glance at the offender. The slight woman sitting anxiously by a young woman's bed looks up at me and I offer a thin smile.

"Opium?" I ask.

"How did you know?" she says, "is it a favourite?"

"No, no, on the contrary." I tuck the tissue up my sleeve, sniffling all the while. "My mum used to wear it all the time before we discovered I was allergic."

"Oh, I am sorry." Her smile is warm, but her eyes are full of sadness.

I've become familiar with most of the faces in the ward since Ivy's been here but they must've admitted this new patient in last night.

"Don't worry," I say, gesturing towards the daffodils on the windowsill, "I've got lots of allergies."

"Is that your mum?" she asks softly, after a while. I look at Ivy sleeping peacefully.

"No," I sigh, "Ivy's my neighbour." Then explain briefly that she's not in for anything serious and doesn't have any family that live nearby.

"Are you related?" I close my magazine and nod at the patient. Her face is red and swollen but I can see a slight resemblance, they must be sisters.

"Yes," she whispers, gazing at the patient adoringly, "Kate's my daughter. A rush of sadness mingled with envy whisks through me at the sight of mother and daughter in unison.

"You look so young," I say, touching my face and thinking of Danny's comment this morning.

"These are new," he said, pointing at my face as we lay tangled in white bedsheets.

"What?" My hand shot to my forehead, "more wrinkles?"

He laughed, told me they were cute, that they gave me character. As did the fine lines around my eyes he'd mentioned the previous week and my thinning lips the week before. "You could have a bit of Botox if it bothers you," he added, "Lots of women your age have it done."

Funnily, I hadn't actually spotted any real signs of aging until I met him and now I can't seem to think of anything else.

I give the visitor's face a quick scan. I wonder if she's had any work done. If she has it's very good.

She looks brilliant for a mum of that thirty-something looking woman lying battered and bruised in that bed.

"Thank you," the visitor sniffs, "but I don't feel it." There's a moment of silence. "She's been in an accident," she says unexpectedly. "Slipped and fell down the stairs. Apparently." She waves a hand. "She's lost the baby. Again. She'll be devastated when she wakes up, that's if...."

"I'm sorry," I offer. "I'm sure she'll be fine. They're very good in here." I gaze around me, "Perhaps her partner should tell her about the baby. It might be better coming from him."

The visitor looks mortified, tells me that she doesn't want him anywhere near Kate. Clearly, she's not keen on her daughter's partner either. It must be a mum thing.

"Please tell me you're joking, Tess," Mum cried last week when I told her that Danny and I were planning a spring wedding.

"Oh, don't tell me, he's too young," I said, hands on hips. "Change the record, Mum, I'm sick of hearing it."

"Amongst other things, yes," she said indignantly. "Ten years might seem like nothing to you now you're only thirty-six but wait until you hit fifty. And don't think that I can't see through that makeup you've plastered on your face to camouflage all that bruising under your eyes. I wasn't born yesterday. And what's this?" She reached for my face, "has he given you a fat lip?" she asked accusingly.

"Oh, Mum, stop it," I pushed her hand away from my face. "I had a bit of an accident, that's all, the other day while I was trying to get some stuff down from the loft." I didn't tell her that I had collagen injected into my lips that very morning. That I'd become a regular at the beauty salon, desperately trying to turn back the clock.

"If you say so," she replied, eyes not leaving mine. "He pushes you around, doesn't he? Lord knows what he'll be like once you're married."

"Oh, don't be ridiculous, Mum." I pulled my cardigan around me tightly. "Look, if you can't be happy for us then just go!" I regret the words the moment they slipped from my lips but it was too late. She leapt to her feet, marched to her car and sped off in a huff, complaining all the while. We haven't spoken since.

Ivy stirs in her bed.

"Hello, love," she manages. "Have you been here long?"

"Nah," I say brightly, "only about ten minutes."

"I don't want to keep you. Danny can't be happy with you sitting by my bedside every night?"

"He's at the gym." I look away and start tidying her bed, tucking the sheets in firmly at the sides, anything to avoid eye contact.

"Again?" she exclaims, and my heart sinks. It's been every night this week. "Any news from your mum?" She coughs and covers her mouth. I shake my head biting hard on my lips to curb the tears from spilling from my eyes. "Make it up with her, love. She only wants what's best for you."

"Don't strain, Ivy, you just rest for a while." And she nods and closes her eyes.

"Sorry," says the visitor, "I couldn't help overhearing. Are you okay?"

"Me?" I ask, surprised. I look at my watch as I walk over to her. We're the last two visitors on the ward. "Yeah, I'm fine." I swallow back the tears but they eventually win and run uncontrollably down my face. And the next thing I know I'm pouring my heart out to this stranger.

I tell her about my fallout with Mum over Danny; how she tried to apologise later that evening but I was too upset to pick up the phone, too pigheaded to reply to her apologetic voicemails. I was even too angry to respond to her texts the following day, and now the silence is just growing and growing. "Oh, I dunno," I say, plaintively, "maybe Mum's right about Danny. All I seem to do is try to please him these days. It's all about the looks with Danny, he's very into all that image stuff."

"Well, I know all about bullying men." She glances at Kate.

"Oh, no." I shake my head vigorously, touching my cheek, "He doesn't hurt me. I just had a bit of Botox and fillers and it's bruised a bit."

"Really?" She smiles softly, "He doesn't have to use his fists to hurt you, you know." She jabs at her temple, "He's got into your head." I frown thoughtfully as I pluck a tissue from the box on Kate's bedside table and blow my nose. A blue-uniformed nurse rustles along, stops, asks if I'm okay. I know that my mascara has run and that I no doubt look like an Alice Cooper tribute act, but I don't care.

"I will have to ask you to leave soon," she tells us, "visiting time is almost over." We nod in unison. "Five more minutes," she whispers.

"I know us mums can seem interfering," the visitor goes on as we gaze at the nurse heading off down the ward, her shoes squeaking against the vinyl floor. "But it's only because we...." She trails off as Kate starts to mumble.

"Mummy?" Kate mutters, drifting in and out of consciousness.

"Darling, can you hear me?" the woman asks urgently, then looks at me, eyes wide. "She can hear me!"

"That's wonderful," I say.

"Where's my husband?" Kate murmurs. "Where's Mike?"

"Kate, you've got to leave him this time, do you hear?" But her eyes close and she drifts back into a deep sleep.

"I suppose I'd better go." The visitor gets to her feet. "Give mum a call, love, won't you. Try and make it up with her. She only sticks her oar in because she cares. Us mum's never stop worrying about our kids, no matter how old they are." I nod as I pull on my jacket. I know she's right.

"You look pleased with yourself," says Ivy, the next morning when I breeze into the ward.

"I called Mum last night," I say brightly, pulling up a chair. "We had a heart to heart, spoke for hours." I can't conceal my excitement.

"That's wonderful news, Tess."

"And I've called it off with Danny."

"Oh, love, I am sorry."

"It's okay, I don't think we're right for each other, Ivy. I can see that now."

There's a dishevelled man by Kate's bedside. They seem to be arguing. Ivy raises her thin, white eyebrows.

91

"Poor lamb has been crying all morning," she whispers. Then suddenly the ward is heaving with commotion.

"Just go, Mike!" Kate yells.

At first, he retaliates, but somehow the nurses manage to calm him and he leaves, mumbling obscenities under his breath. Ivy and I exchange glances as her consultant and his team bustle onto the ward, pulling the curtains around Ivy's bed nosily. I wait outside.

"Sorry, was that your husband?" I walk towards Kate.

"Err.. do I know you?" Kate squints at me.

"No, I...." I falter. "It's just that I overheard you asking after him yesterday and..."

"So, you heard that, did you?" she cuts in, "Oh, don't look so worried" Kate hoists herself up in bed. "I was dreaming about Hope." I frown. "My mum."

"Oh, it wasn't a drea....."

"She's been dead for twenty years." Her cut lip quivers. "I must've been talking in my sleep again."

"Oh." My hand flies to my chest. I stare into space in a daze. I can hear the buzzing of a radio, nurses chatting, phones bleeping, but I can't seem to focus.

"Are you okay?" Kate's voice again. "Hello? Shall I call a nurse?"

"No, no, I'm fine. Sorry. I just had a bit of a dizzy spell, that's all."

And with a frown Kate nods. "I often dream about mum when I'm in trouble. I can almost smell her sometimes. Hear her voice.....so clearly, almost as if....."

"She was right here," I finish, taking in a deep breath of hospital scented air fused with a hint of Opium and sneezing twice.

I HEART YOU

The scent of essential oils wafts delightfully under my nose as I step into the foamy water. Martin has taken the kids to the local park, which gives me two hours of *me* time before my fortieth birthday party. I want to look my best, especially as I'm about to come face to face with my husband's lover.

I recline into the hot, steaming bath, but as I close my eyes Martin and Laura spring into my mind and my stomach twists. I'm walking towards their workstation. It's one of those open plan offices with glass partitions. He wasn't expecting me, of course, it was a surprise visit. I thought we'd go out for lunch or grab a coffee, spend a bit of quality time together while the kids were at school. But as I approached his section, all smiles and anticipation, I saw her silently mouth those three sacred words to him. *'I love you'.*

My heart slumped into my stomach. Laura was tall, slender and gorgeous, and did I mention young? But instead of bursting in and demanding to know what was going on, I spun on my heel and ran and ran and ran as fast as my legs could carry me.

At the lift, I pressed all the buttons at once in a frenzy before racing down the stairs. I had to get out and fast. When the fresh air hit me, the shock was quickly replaced by a sudden feeling of dread. I was about to lose my husband.

That evening, I let Martin fall asleep on the sofa, as usual, then searched his pockets for evidence - hotel receipts, posh restaurant bills, hotel invoices. But there was nothing. He was hiding his tracks well, Martin's a clever man, I expected no less.

"There's only one thing for it," said my friend Susie when I'd confided my worries to her the next morning. "Invite her to your fortieth and see how they are together."

I refused to begin with. I mean, it was a bit over the top, wasn't it? And what excuse could I give Martin, but eventually she twisted my arm, and I agreed. He seemed to take it in his stride the next day when I asked him to invite his colleagues to my party. In fact, he even suggested firing up the barbeque.

I tie the belt of my dressing gown tightly at my waist. There's a tap at the door, then Martin's voice, "Nancy, we're back." I open the door. "Phew, what's that smell?" he asks, mist steaming up his glasses.

"Bath oils, they're supposed to be romantic." He raises his eyebrows. "So, is Laura bringing anyone," I say nonchalantly, combing my wet hair in front of the mirror.

"Her boyfriend, I think," he buffs his glasses.

"Boyfriend?"

"Well, don't sound so surprised. She's quite popular, lots of men fancy her." One of them being you, I want to say, but I don't. Instead, I push him away gently and scurry off to our bedroom.

"What's up?" His footsteps creak against the landing behind me. "I thought you were looking forward to tonight."

I stop and face him. "Martin, do you still love me?"

He looks at me, dumbfounded. "What? Course, I do." He gives his glasses a final buff before slipping them back on, "What's brought this on?"

"It's just that you never say it."

"I do!" he says indignantly.

"No, Martin, you say I heart you."

"Same difference."

"No, it's not. I...Oh...never mind. I need to get ready."

My party's a success. Laura's boyfriend, Max, is gorgeous. In fact, he's been giving me flirtatious glances all evening. So, after a few glasses of wine, I don't resist when he pulls me onto the dance floor. I glance at Martin and Laura, their faces like thunder. But I've no intention of taking things further. I've never been petty or vindictive and I'm not about to start now. I thank Max and head for the kitchen.

"What's the matter with you?" demands Martin, following me briskly, "You're making a spectacle of yourself."

"It's a party, Martin, I'm enjoying myself," I say. And then, out of nowhere I hear myself say, "At least I'm not shagging my colleague."

"What?" he asks incredulously.

"Don't deny it. I saw Laura telling you she loved you in your office a couple of weeks ago." I brace myself but he laughs and shakes his head.

"Is that why you ran from the office? I did see you, you know. I came after you but the lift had already gone down."

"Why didn't you come looking for me?"

"Nancy, I thought you'd talk to me about it."

"So you're not denying it then?" I ask, tearfully, tearing a paper hand towel to shreds.

"Look, it's not how it seems." I follow his eyes to Laura who's appeared at the door, glass in hand.

"Sorry, hope I'm not interrupting anything," she says, tentatively.

"No, come on in," I yell, "You're practically part of our family anyway." My heart is pounding against my ribcage.

"Nancy!" Martin blushes, apologises to Laura. Why is he trying to protect her? He must really care for her. I feel sick.

"Laura and I are not having an affair," Martin says firmly.

"An affair?" Laura looks horrified.

"She saw you tell me you loved me." Laura frowns. "Monday before last," he goes on, "Well, she thinks you did."

Laura frowns and then her eyes light up, "Oh, yeah," she snorts, "The password."

"Password?" I repeat, wiping my nose with what's left of the kitchen towel.

"Laura and I share an account. It's a Graphic Design company called Grey Koo. We are the only two who know the password to get into the system." He sighs and looks at Laura. "I forgot the wretched thing and Laura mouthed it to me so that no one else could hear."

"Elephant Koo," Laura finishes.

"Hey?" I'm confused. Martin takes me by the hand and leads me to the mirror in the hallway.

"Say, *Elephant Koo* silently." As I do, the words 'I love you' form on my lips.

"I thought you were going to leave us?" I say quietly.

"Nancy, I'd never leave my family. I love you too much." I'm in his arms and he's squeezing me tightly, securely.

Feeling like a complete twat, I mouth, "*I'm sorry*" to Laura over Martin's shoulder.

"No worries," Laura smiles, "I'd better go, Max is waiting." I nod, smiling. "See you on Monday, Martin."

Martin acknowledges her with a lazy arm wave as he rocks me gently in his arms, and just at that moment I swear I see a mist of heartbreak in her eyes.

Printed in Great Britain
by Amazon